Duke

Best Friends Series
Book 4

David M. Sargent, Jr. and his friends all live in a small town in northwest Arkansas. While he lies in the hammock, the dogs (left to right: Spike, Emma, Daphne and Mary) play ball, dig holes or bark at kitty cats. When not playing in the yard, they travel around the United States, meeting children and writing stories.

Duke

Best Friends Series
Book 4

David M. Sargent, Jr.

Illustrated by Debbie Farmer

Ozark Publishing, Inc.
P.O. Box 228
Prairie Grove, AR 72753

Cataloging-in-Publication Data

Sargent, David M., 1966–
    Duke / by David M. Sargent, Jr. ;
illustrated by Debbie Farmer.—Prairie Grove, AR :
Ozark Publishing, c2007.
      p. cm. (Best friends series ; 4)

    "Friends"—Cover.
    SUMMARY: When Dalton and Steve race
to the river, they fall on the green grass, laughing.
Duke jumps to a rock in the edge of the water.
It looks like fun! Steve tries it. But something
goes wrong. His feet fly out from under him and
he falls into the deep water. When he remembers
that he can't swim, he panics!
    ISBN 1-59381-064-4 (hc)
           1-59381-065-2 (pbk)

    1. Dogs—Juvenile fiction.
[1. Dogs—Fiction. 2. Collies—Fiction.]
I. Farmer, Debbie, 1958– ill. II. Title.
III. Series.

    PZ8.3.S2355Du 2007
    [E]—dc21   2003099200

Printed in the United States of America

iv

Inspired by

a Collie dog my mama had when she was a young girl.

Dedicated to

all children who love fluffy Collies.
They are very intelligent dogs.

Foreword

When Dalton and Steve race to the river, they fall on the green grass, laughing. Duke jumps to a rock in the edge of the water. It looks like fun! Steve tries it. But something goes wrong. His feet fly out from under him and he falls into the deep water. When he remembers that he can't swim, he panics!

Contents

If you would like to have the author of the Best Friends Series visit your school free of charge, please call 1-800-321-5671.

One

Race to the Creek

Dalton and his friend Steve ran through the woods toward the creek. Duke, Dalton's Collie, raced ahead of them, chasing birds and squirrels.

Dalton laughed at the Collie. "Duke, you are one crazy dog. You never catch anything. Why don't you just give up?"

Duke ran back to Dalton. He licked his hand, and then another bird landed nearby.

A bark and a leap later, he was darting toward it. The boys watched the bird fly into the nearest tree.

"Old Duke is a neat dog, Dalton," Steve said. "But he isn't much good for nothing but chasing birds and squirrels."

"He is, too!" Dalton replied.
"He's worth a whole lot more than
your old mutt."

Steve glared at him, but Dalton ignored it.

"Maybe we'll see a deer when we get to the creek," he muttered.

"Yeah," his friend grumbled.
"Maybe so."

The boys grinned at each other.

"I'll race you to the creek!"
Dalton said. They took off!

Two

Don't Play Near Water

The boys raced toward the water's edge at a dead run. They fell onto the grassy bank, laughing.

Duke sat down nearby, cocking his head from side to side, as he looked at them.

"I'm glad it's Saturday," Steve said. "I had to study hard all week for that math test we had yesterday. I'm ready for a break."

"Me too," Dalton grunted. "I think I passed it, but I'm not sure."

"Me too," Steve said. "We can play all day today."

"Not quite," Dalton replied. "Mom told me to be home early. She said Sally and her mother are coming for a visit."

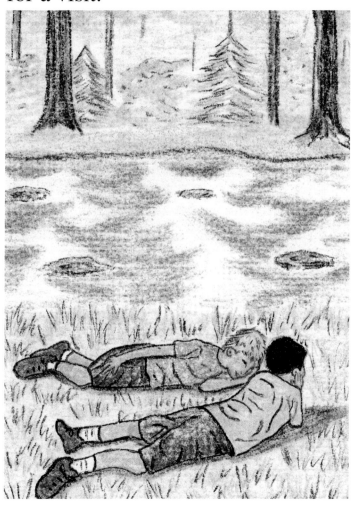

Dalton wrinkled his nose. "Mom wants me to play with Sally while she talks to Sally's mom."

"Sally sounds like a girl. Yuck!" Steve gasped. "You mean you have to play with a girl?"

"Yeah," Dalton said. "Worse than going to school, huh?"

Steve saw Duke leap onto a rock in the creek.

"Hey, Duke," he shouted. "That looks like fun. Come on, Dalton!"

Three

A Fall into Deep Water

Steve ran to the water's edge and leaped onto a rock. His feet flew out from under him, and he fell into the deep water.

"H-H-Help!" he shouted. "Help me, Dalton! I can't swim!"

Dalton ran toward Steve, but Duke leaped in front of him and growled.

"Get out of the way, Duke!" he screamed. "Steve's drowning!"

Duke's teeth snapped together as he took a step toward Dalton. The boy fell over backward and landed on the grass. Duke whirled and looked toward the creek.

"H-H-Help!" Steve gasped. As he disappeared below the surface, Duke leaped into the water.

Seconds later, he pulled Steve onto the bank.

"Are you okay?" Dalton asked.
Steve coughed hard and then
sputtered. Finally he sat up.

Steve hugged Duke and said, "You saved my life, Duke. I'm sorry for the mean things I said. You can chase all the birds and squirrels you want to."

"Duke," Dalton said as he hugged the dog's neck. "I'm so proud of you! You're my best friend."